OTHER YEARLING BOOKS YOU WILL ENJOY:

YEARLING BOOKS/YOUNG YEARLINGS/YEARLING CLASSICS are designed especially to entertain and enlighten young people. Patricia Reilly Giff, consultant to this series, received her bachelor's degree from Marymount College and a master's degree in history from St. John's University. She holds a Professional Diploma in Reading and a Doctorate of Humane Letters from Hofstra University. She was a teacher and reading consultant for many years, and is the author of numerous books for young readers.

For a complete listing of all Yearling titles, write to Dell Readers Service, P.O. Box 1045, South Holland, IL 60473.

Dunc and Amos Hit the Big Top

Gary Paulsen

Dunc and Amos Hit the Big Top

A YEARLING BOOK

Published by
Dell Publishing
a division of
Bantam Doubleday Dell Publishing Group, Inc.
666 Fifth Avenue
New York, New York 10103

ISBN: 0-440-40756-7

Printed in the United States of America

February 1993

10 9 8 7 6 5 4 3 2 1

OPM

Dunc and Amos Hit the Big Top

Chapter·1

Dunc folded the newspaper neatly, exactly as it had been folded when it was fresh, and placed it on his desk carefully, the edge of the paper lined up with the edge of the desk. Then he rearranged his pencil holder—an old distributor cap off a car—so that the older pencils, the shorter ones, were in front and the longer new ones were in the rear. . .

"Stop it!" Amos, his truly best friend for life, except for the time Dunc made Amos go hang-gliding and they got lost in a wilderness area and Amos was rich but grabbed a can of Spam instead of a bar of gold—Amos couldn't stand it when Dunc was being neat.

1

"You've been fiddling with that desk and stuff for hours and hours."

"No," Dunc said, looking at his watch. "Altogether I spend about thirty-five seconds a day straightening my desk, and by rough calculations that thirty-five seconds saves me nearly seventy-four minutes through the day because I don't have to hunt for things—"

"I'm going to strangle you."

"—the way you have to search for things. Besides, what does it matter how much time I spend straightening my desk?"

Amos moved to the desk and picked up the paper, jerked it open, ripped a page loose (Dunc winced at the sound of the tearing paper), and held it out to Dunc. "This is why it matters."

Dunc took the page of paper and scanned it. "It's an advertisement. So what?"

Amos looked at the ceiling, started to think of a word to say that he'd seen written on a locker in the gym, then sighed. "What is it an advertisement for?"

Dunc shrugged. "A circus."

Amos shook his head. "No, Dunc—not just

a circus. This is *the* circus. This is the annual Chamber of Commerce circus."

Dunc shrugged again. "Like I said, so what? A bunch of tacky costumes and bored animals and stale popcorn. We go every year, and every year it's the same thing."

Amos shook his head. "Not this time. This time, if you had taken the extra moment to read the small print at the bottom of the ad, you would have found that they are going to include a special section for amateur talent."

Dunc nodded. "I read that. So?"

"Man—sometimes you are so dense. So every year Melissa goes to the circus, and I have been trying to get her to notice me."

Dunc nodded again. Amos had long ago decided that Melissa Hansen was pretty much the cosmic center of the universe as he'd come to know it, and she pretty much didn't think of him at all. Ever.

"So," Amos said. "I've signed up for the amateur talent night at the circus. Melissa will be sitting right down front, and there I'll be, right out there where she can't miss me."

"Amos . . ."

"On the trapeze."

"The trapeze?"

Amos smiled. "You bet—I need something that shows, something great. I figured the trapeze was the best way to go. I thought about lion taming, but I'm not sure they'll let you in with the lions—you know, if you're an amateur."

"Trapeze?" Dunc repeated, shaking his head slowly. "Amos, you can't be serious."

"Dead serious."

"That might be exactly what it comes to—dead. Amos, you just got the neck brace off, or have you forgotten last week?"

Amos rubbed his neck. "No. I haven't forgotten."

"That was in the privacy of your own home, your own room—what will it be like on a trapeze?"

Amos held up his hand. "That was a fluke."

"You were answering the phone and almost killed yourself."

Amos rolled his neck from side to side and shook his head. "That isn't quite right. I was *trying* to answer the phone, and I had a little accident."

"Little accident? You totaled the house!"

"No—it wasn't even close to the whole house. More just the kitchen and the back porch and part of the garage and the trash cans in the alley." He paused, remembering.

Amos was always certain Melissa was going to call, and he always tried to get to the phone by the end of the first ring.

And never made it.

This had been a classic case of phone answering. Amos had been walking down the hallway that led off the front door to the house when he heard the phone ring.

Many things happened when the phone rang in Amos's house. First, anybody and everybody in the house froze where they were in terror, wondering if they were in the line of travel between Amos and the nearest phone. This included Scruff, the family dog, who had been run over so many times, he almost no longer bit Amos when he went by.

In Amos's mind the ringing phone triggered a whole different set of responses. First, as the ring started, almost automatically his legs began to pump, driving him into a run before he really knew which direction to move. Second, within a split instant, his brain registered the closest phone ringing—his father had no less than four phones in the house (he kept increasing the number as the disasters occurred)—and the direction and exact distance to the phone.

All this happened in the first second.

It was during the second second that things usually began to fall apart, and this time had been no exception.

He'd had good form, almost classic, knees pumping, tongue out the side of his mouth, a good lungful of air for the start.

But he'd been going in the wrong direction when the phone rang.

Dunc had tried to explain inertia to him many times. A body in motion tends to stay in motion; every action has an equal and opposite reaction.

But applying it was always hard for Amos, and he'd made two good pumps, his hand out for the phone, when his brain ordered him to turn and go the other way.

The top half of his body began the turn, but his legs took one more step before swinging around, and in that step he came down on

6

Scruff, who had stopped dead in the middle of the hallway when the phone rang.

Scruff reacted normally, violently. He started down with Amos on his back and reached up and around and grabbed Amos's foot, catching a fang in the looped end of Amos's shoelace, then cutting sideways to get out of the way.

The fang pulled the shoelace with it, and the shoelace pulled the shoe, and the shoe pulled the foot, and the foot pulled the leg.

Like falling dominoes, Amos came over and down.

Except that he was still moving in full stride, his body still propelled forward, and his eyes widened in horror as he saw he was aimed at the center of the kitchen table, where his mother was busy preparing a snack after a hard day at work. She was holding a butcher knife.

She turned, her own eyes widening to see a careening pile of boy and dog and shoes coming at her end over end. She moved deftly sideways, throwing the knife into the sink to get it out of the way just in time for Amos and Scruff to hit the table, driving it through the kitchen and onto the back porch, through the back porch and out across the small back yard into the trash barrels, swiping the trim off the side of the garage as they passed.

On the way by, Amos had snagged the phone from the hook, and he held it to his ear in the middle of the pile of wreckage in the alley, Scruff still hanging on his foot. He said: "Hello?"

But the wire had torn from the wall, and he'd been talking to nobody.

"No," he said now, remembering, "it wasn't the whole house at all. Now, let's go to the circus—I've got to sign up for the trapeze."

Chapter · 2

The circus was on the edge of town and was almost not a circus. At one time it had been a big, three-ring spectacular show—but that had been back in the fifties.

It was down now to a tired bigtop tent with patches here and there and a few animal cages and a bunch of men that Dunc thought either had been in prison, should be in prison, or would be in prison soon.

But it *was* a circus, and Amos's nostrils flared with excitement as they chained their bicycles to a telephone pole and locked them.

Dunc stopped at the rope-gate area leading into the circus compound and held Amos back.

"Amos, I'm not certain this is a good idea—actually, I'm positive that it's a bad idea."

Amos stopped and turned to Dunc. "Oh, sure—every time you have an idea it's a good idea, and every time I have an idea it's a bad one. Well, let's just review things a bit, shall we? Who did the hang-gliding disaster, me or you?"

Dunc hesitated.

"Come on."

"Me. But—"

"And whose idea was it to mess with a stinking old parrot and look for buried treasure?"

"Well . . ."

"Whose?"

"All right, that was me too."

Amos nodded. "I think you'll find that most of the ideas that have led to our nearly dying came from you. So this time let me have an idea."

"But Amos—there are people here who haven't had a bath since last year."

Amos shrugged. "So what? You've always spent way too much time on hygiene. It might do you good to get a little dirty."

Amos left Dunc standing with his mouth open, turned, and went through the gate. Or tried to.

A thin man—Dunc thought he probably hadn't eaten anything in a week—held out a gray hand. "Wait a minute, kid—where you going?"

Amos had the clipping from the paper about the amateur talent. "I'm here for the amateur talent event."

"What part?"

"The trapeze."

The man studied Amos for a long time, then shook his head. "I don't know. A lot of kids are trying to get in free by using that amateur thing."

Amos drew his shoulders up. "I'm not lying —I'm an expert tumbler and gymnast. Ask my friend." He motioned back to Dunc.

The man looked at Dunc.

Dunc stared at Amos. As far as he knew, Amos had never tried gymnastics or tumbling in his life. Unless you counted the times answering the telephone.

Amos turned and stared back at Dunc.

Dunc nodded.

11

"Well . . . " The man still hesitated, unconvinced, but a second man came up to him. If anything he was grayer and thinner than the first, and he had a lit cigarette with a long ash hanging from the corner of his mouth.

"Come on, B.J.—let's get some food down. I've only got twenty minutes before I have to dress up for the geek show."

B.J. waved Amos past. "All right. You can go in, but your friend has to have a ticket. You get it over there." He pointed to a small booth at the side of the entrance.

"I'm not buying a ticket for this," Dunc said to Amos, turning to leave. "Why should I pay to watch you die? I can come and watch you answer the phone for nothing."

Amos grabbed his arm. "Come on—I'll pay for the ticket."

And finally, Dunc leaving skid marks with his heels, Amos bought him a ticket and dragged him into the big top.

Inside the tent it was cool and dark and almost completely insane with noise and movement. It was close to noon, and the first show of the day started at four o'clock, and even Dunc could see they would be lucky to make it.

One crew was trying to erect an animal cage in the big center—and only—ring but there were just four men, and they seemed to be spending most of their time running in circles and swearing at each other.

"Reminds me of the parrot," Amos said. "The language, I mean."

Dunc nodded. "I've even heard some new ones."

"I wonder who's in charge?" Amos asked.

"From the way it looks, nobody."

One of the men working on the ring saw the boys and yelled at them. "Don't just stand there—come on, take a strain!"

His voice was like a whip, and Dunc and Amos were moving before they thought to question it. Amos grabbed a section of the cage and tried to lift it, but it was too heavy, so Dunc helped him. No sooner did they have it up than another man came and pulled it down.

"Not yet—it's too soon."

"Too soon for what?" Amos asked.

"Too soon to put the cage up, dummy."

"Oh."

"We don't want to do it too soon, or they'll start expecting it."

"Oh."

"Didn't they tell you anything when they hired you on as rousts?"

Amos shook his head. "Nope."

The man turned and walked away to tip over another section of cage that two other hands were raising. "Not yet—it's too soon."

Dunc whispered to Amos. "We're not hired on as rousts."

"Who cares? If they think we work here, we can move around easier. Come on, let's find somebody who knows about the talent contest."

Amos moved away from the ring and into the back of the tent, near where a small stand had been erected for the band, except that there wasn't a band. Instead there were two men with trumpets and a set of drums that looked as if they'd been used in the Civil War.

The two men could have been twins. They were both short, round, and bald and had bellies hanging over their belts. They were dressed in tired suits, and one of them was tightening the head on a snare drum.

"Hi," Amos said. "We're looking for somebody in charge."

Both men looked up at the same time. "That's funny, you don't look like a bill collector."

"I'm not—I'm here to sign up for the amateur talent event."

"Ah, Willy, he's here for the amateur talent event," the man on the drum said to the other.

"Yes, Billy, I heard that. Tell me, young man, what event do you wish to work in?"

Amos coughed. "The trapeze."

"Ah, Willy, he wants to do the trapeze . . ."

"I heard that, Billy." He turned to Amos. "Is it possible, young man, that you have had some experience on the trapeze?"

Amos nodded. "Oh, yes. I've been—trapezing—for a long time. It's a hobby, and it's always been my dream to work in a circus, flying around from swing to swing, wearing tights."

"Ah, Willy, he's had experience. . . ."

Willy nodded. "I heard that, Billy."

"So if you'll just tell us where to find the man in charge," Amos said, "we'll sign up and get ready for the show."

"Ah, Willy, he wants to see the man in charge."

"Yes, Billy, I heard. Well, you see, young man, it would seem that you're speaking to him. Or them. We own the circus. Or we will until the bill collectors take it from us, which they have been trying to do for years."

"Oh. Well then, where do I sign?"

"There's a problem with that," Willy said. "We are fresh out of trapeze acts at the moment for you to work with as amateur talent."

"Yes," Billy said. "Fresh out."

"It would seem," Willy said, "that the Great Spangliny had an attack of good sense and last night left before his bluff was called."

"Bluff?" Amos asked.

"Yes. The Great Spangliny had talked, no, bragged about doing his most death-defying and gravity-cheating performance this very evening."

"What was he going to do?" Dunc cut in.

"A solo-four somersault forward dive from

one bar to another, with both bars swinging in full arcs."

"Wow."

"Yes." Billy nodded, sighing. "It would have made the show." He looked at Amos. "But now I'm afraid it's all off. Spangliny is gone—left this morning."

"When you say 'gone' "—Amos rubbed his chin—"how do you mean that?"

"Gone. He pulled out this morning."

"Did he take all his equipment?"

Billy shook his head. "No. We own the equipment. He just left a note saying he thought he'd try brain surgery for a while and pinned the note to my door."

Dunc had been quiet all this time, but he looked intently at Amos and shook his head. "No, Amos."

Amos ignored him and spoke to Billy. "So all the equipment is still here, and you just need somebody to jump around to have a show, right?"

Billy sighed. "Exactly. We need a trapeze artist."

"No, you don't," Amos said. "I'll do it."

"No." Dunc held up his hand. "Amos, don't do this."

Amos smiled at Billy. "Would you excuse us for a moment?"

He turned and dragged Dunc back out of earshot. "What are you trying to do—kill the whole deal?"

Dunc nodded. "Yes. Are you completely insane?"

Amos looked at the top of the tent, then back down to Dunc. "Don't you see? This is my best chance ever to get Melissa to see me. There she'll be, sitting in the audience, and I'll be in center ring with the spotlights on me."

"*Above* center ring," Dunc corrected. "*Way* above."

"So?"

"If you fall—"

"I'm not going to fall. Remember, you're the one who dragged me umpteen million miles dangling from a hang-glider. This is nothing—plus, there'll be a net. Just a minute."

Amos turned and trotted over to Billy. "There's a net, right?"

18

Billy nodded. "A good one."

Amos trotted back to Dunc. "So there's a net. Even if I fall, I'll just bounce a little."

Dunc shook his head again. "It's still crazy. You've never been on a trapeze in your life, and you're going to do a quadruple somersault?"

"Don't be silly. I can't do that. I'll just swing around a little while in the spotlights and make sure Melissa sees me, then do a death-defying drop into the net, and that ought to about do it. She'll be mine."

"What's left of you."

"Don't worry," Amos said over his shoulder as he moved back to Billy and Willy. "It can't go wrong."

Chapter · 3

Willy and Billy had not been easy to convince.

"There's the insurance," Willy had said.

"And your bones," Billy had said. "There are so many to break."

Finally, after what seemed hours to Dunc and days to Amos, the two owners had consented to Amos's scheme to perform as the solo trapeze artist.

"*If,*" Willy had insisted, "you show us what you can do on the trapeze and work with us for the next few hours until showtime."

"Work?" Amos had been turning away and he stopped. "What do you mean, work?"

"Help us set up," Willy said.

"Yes," Billy nodded. "Help us set up. We always seem to have trouble setting up, don't we, Willy?"

"Oh my, do we. Setting up is one of our most difficult parts. Along with selling tickets and keeping track of the money and doing the show and taking it down, I should add. And of course, traveling."

"Ah yes." Billy sighed. "There's the traveling. We always seem to have trouble with that as well, don't we?"

"We certainly do."

Dunc stepped forward. "Is there a part of the circus, you know, that you don't have trouble with?"

Willy rubbed his chin, thinking. "Well, now that you mention it, no—we seem to have trouble with just about everything, don't we, Billy?"

Billy rubbed his chin in exactly the same way. "Now that I think of it, you're right there, too. We seem to have difficulties with everything, don't we?"

"We'll be glad to help you," Dunc said. "We have to go home and change into work clothes."

Dunc turned and left. Amos followed with a bewildered look on his face.

"What was that all about?" Amos asked as they approached their bicycles.

"What do you mean?"

"One minute you're trying to stop me, and the next minute you're volunteering us for work with the circus."

Dunc smiled, wide-eyed and innocent-looking. "I thought you wanted to get involved with the circus."

"Not like this—not with work. I just wanted to be the trapeze artist and get Melissa's attention. I didn't want to *work*."

Dunc unlocked and straddled his bike and flicked the shift lever into second gear and kicked off and started pedaling. He never started in low unless he was starting up an almost vertical hill. He said it was too inefficient. As always, Amos started in low and stayed there too long before he shifted—until his legs and feet were a blur trying to catch up with Dunc.

"You've got to pay your dues," Dunc said.

"What dues?" Amos shifted but went too far, got the lever into fourth, and had to click it back and forth several times to hit second and then third.

"Your dues to be a star." Dunc coasted for a moment. "You've got to work to learn the circus business before you can be a star."

Amos stared at him. "Are you nuts? I just want to swing on the trapeze bar a few times and get Melissa to call me. You sound like my father, with all this dues stuff. He's always saying I've got to settle down and pay my dues and learn and study and get ready for college."

Dunc wiggled a finger at Amos. "He's right, Amos. You've got to settle down and pay your dues and work."

Dunc kicked down hard and pedaled ahead before Amos could see him smiling.

Chapter • 4

Dunc and Amos were in Dunc's room. Dunc was sitting on the footlocker at the foot of the bed, and Amos was sitting at Dunc's desk, wondering at the neatness. His own room looked as if it were hit daily by a hurricane. In Dunc's room nothing, not a thing, was ever out of place or mussed. Amos was idly wheeling a Rolodex, watching the cards flop. "Man, you've even got me on this thing—don't you know my number by heart yet?"

Dunc had been writing on a piece of blank paper on a clipboard, and he stopped the pencil and looked up. "What?"

"You have me on the Rolodex—don't you know my number by heart yet?"

"Sure, why?"

"*BECAUSE YOU HAVE ME ON THE ROLODEX!*" Amos spun the Rolodex. "You haven't heard a word I said—what's the matter with you?"

Dunc went back to the clipboard. "I'm working on this circus problem."

Amos leaned over to see the paper. "What circus problem?"

"The whole thing." Dunc held the clipboard up. "It doesn't make sense."

Amos studied the paper. It was covered with numbers and abbreviations and equations. "You're right there," Amos said. "I can't make head or tail of it. What does 'Wk. plus Csh. equals S.' mean?"

"It's a formula for business. It means work plus cash—money—equals success."

"Oh. Stupid of me not to see that. Here I was, thinking I ought to be trying to find some tights for my trapeze act tonight, but I should have been thinking of a formula for business."

"Well think of it, Amos." Dunc held up the paper again. "Any business works that way.

But if you apply it to the circus, it isn't working."

"What do you mean?"

"The circus has people working and people coming to watch the shows and spending money on tickets, but they aren't having success."

Amos nodded. "So?"

"So why doesn't the equation work? That's what's bugging me."

"And that's why you said we'd come and work. Not because of me, but because you think there's a mystery here?"

"Well—"

"You just can't leave it alone, can you?" Amos snorted. "You're going to get us in another mess I just know it."

"Me?" Dunc threw the clipboard on the bed. "You're the one who wanted to kill himself on the trapeze. I just happened to be there."

"Great, just great—you'll mess this one all up, too. Every time I get a chance to do something that will get Melissa to notice me, you come along and booger it up. All I need is some kind of costume to make me look good, and you're off on one of your mysteries. It's always a mystery. Everything is always a mystery to you. Well just this once, Dunc, just this once, why don't you admit you're wrong and I'm right, and there isn't some big hairy mystery going on that requires clipboards and formulas and—"

Dunc threw his arms in the air. "All right, all right. I'll help you with your costume. But first we have to get back to the circus and get to work."

Dunc motioned to the door, and Amos moved ahead of him out of the room, and Dunc started to follow, but as he reached the door he stopped, turned, went back to the desk, and tore the paper with the formulas off the clipboard, folded it, and put it in his pocket.

Then he followed Amos outside where their bicycles waited.

Chapter · 5

"Those guys were nuts," Amos said.

"What guys?" Dunc paused and looked up.

"The ones who always wrote in books that it was fun to run off with the circus. It's not fun at all."

"Maybe we have to be more patient."

"I've been here two hours, and all I've seen is the wrong end of these animals and this shovel and rake."

"You found out about your costume," Dunc said. "They've got one here in the service truck that will fit you."

"Still. . . ."

They had not been back to the circus for

more than two minutes when the tall, thin, evil-looking man named Clyde but who everybody called Blades—neither of the boys wanted to know about the nickname—had handed them shovels and rakes and pointed to the animal enclosure.

"Willy and Billy said to put you to work—so clean."

"We're supposed to be helping set up," Dunc said.

"It's all the same circus. So pick it up."

It seemed to measure in the tons, and the boys had been busy for over two hours, putting *it* in large plastic bags to stack where a garbage truck would pick *it* up in the evening.

"Man," Dunc said, heaving a sack onto the pile, "think what this would do for Mom's garden."

Amos was looking down at his pants. "A lot more than it does for my clothes. I've got to be honest, I'm not sure even Melissa is worth all this—"

They would argue later over what word, what precise word Amos had been about to use next, but it didn't matter.

What mattered is that at that exact moment a phone rang.

It is true that the phone was a temporary one set up on the side of a power pole strictly for the use of the managers of the circus, true that it was good for local calls only and did not have a public number or even a permanent number, and also true that nearly nobody in town knew it was there, and also true that nobody who knew Amos knew the phone was there, and absolutely positively completely certain that Melissa Hansen didn't know the phone was there, and if she did would not have used it to call Amos.

None of that mattered.

Dunc was convinced that genetic codes were involved and that in Amos's DNA there were ancient phone-answering links that made it impossible for Amos not to answer a phone. No matter where, when, or how—when a phone rang, Amos had to answer it on that all-important first ring because he knew, even when it couldn't possibly be, he *knew* that it was Melissa trying to call him.

"Amos—" Dunc started when the phone rang, but it was too late.

And even then it might have been all right.

The phone on the pole was exactly thirty-seven yards and four inches from where Amos stood, holding the shovel, and while it is not likely that he would have made it on the all-important first ring, he had a good chance of at least coming close, which was as good as he ever did.

And his form was good. Not quite classic, with both legs pumping, knees up by the side of his head, tongue out the corner of the mouth with a little spit flying through the air —not that good, but not too bad.

He dropped the shovel, which was better than he usually did—he once ran into the living room to answer the phone and forgot he was mowing the lawn, taking the mower inside with him.

He dropped the shovel. His ears and brain located the phone to the exact millimeter, noted the quickest possible way to the pole and phone, and his left leg dug, bunched, and propelled him off to the right. His right leg contracted, dug, and pushed off, and in half a second he was at full speed, arrowing straight for the phone as if he were tied on a wire.

Directly under Biboe.

The quickest way to the phone was exactly through the animals and the mess they were cleaning up. There were llamas and camels and some goats for a petting zoo, and three horses and a couple of ostriches and Biboe.

Biboe the elephant.

Biboe had been up and down the river. He was pushing forty years old and had been raised in circuses and lived there the whole time and knew the routines perfectly.

Twice a day he went into the big tent and stood up on his back legs and twirled around with a girl on his head while some guy in a turban yelled at him, and then he came out here and they hosed him down and gave him hay and peanuts.

It worked for Biboe. He did his gig twice a day and sometimes got extra peanuts from kids who came by the petting zoo, and that was how his days went.

More to the point, he didn't like changes. Once the guy with the turban had actually hooked him in back of the ear with the little metal hook he carried just for show, and Biboe had objected so forcefully, it took four men to get the man with the turban out of a garbage can, and he still walked funny and wouldn't go anywhere near the elephant enclosure.

But more than just disliking changes, Biboe hated *rapid* changes. Any sudden movement startled him, and any quick alteration in routine upset Biboe, and an upset Biboe was a problem Biboe.

A problem Biboe that weighed close to four tons.

And a phone ringing, coupled with a shovel and rake dropping to the ground and a boy starting to run, were all elements of rapid change.

Perhaps it still would have worked out all right, except that the straightest line from Amos to the phone went directly beneath Biboe, and without thinking, all on reflex, Amos made for the phone in the shortest possible direction.

Straight under Biboe.

It was too much, far too much. Amos ducked to clear Biboe's hay-full belly, dug with his right foot, and started for the pole with the phone.

But Biboe was faster. Like a striking snake, his trunk whipped back and wrapped around Amos, going under his armpit and back up and around his neck.

"*Gurrrk.*" It was not a word so much as a choke, and it was very nearly the last thing Amos said. Luckily for Amos, there were no garbage cans nearby, or he probably would have gotten stuffed.

"Biboe!" Dunc yelled. "Drop him!"

Biboe ignored Dunc, held Amos for a second, a full six feet off the ground, looked around for a can or Dumpster, and when he could find nothing suitable, he made a couple of swings around in the air and threw Amos away. It was the same gesture he might have used to get rid of rotten hay or bad peanuts.

Except that Amos—still wondering what had happened to him since one second he'd been running for the phone and the next he was hanging by his neck well off the ground— had mass and weight going, and when Biboe threw him, he kind of flipped him as well.

Amos left the animal enclosure in a spiraling forward somersault that took him forty feet into the air, across the open compound, to fall on the roof of the big top almost perfectly flat on his back, where he bounced once, slid down softly and gently, and landed perfectly on his feet.

Directly in front of Billy and Willy, who had not seen Biboe throw him but had seen Amos flying through the air in a perfect forward somersault and a likewise perfect landing on the tent.

"Oh, my," Willy said to Billy. "Isn't he just the one to take Spangliny's place?"

Billy nodded. "Goodness yes. That was simply classic. Young man, you needn't give us a demonstration of your abilities. We've just seen all we need to see."

Amos smiled faintly and tried to nod. In his mind he was still back, walking beneath the elephant and suddenly flying. "Thank you. I think."

On the power pole a circus worker hung up the phone and turned to another worker.

"Wrong number."

Chapter · 6

"I think I'm working it out," Dunc said.

"Working what out?" Amos took a bite of a hot dog with red-hot chili sauce on it. They had finished cleaning the animal enclosure—Amos had moved very carefully around Biboe—and gone to the food trailer for a snack.

Amos chewed the hot dog until the sauce hit his tongue, then drank some Coke, then chewed, then drank. His forehead broke out in sweat and he grimaced, but he kept eating it.

It was part of his theory of life, which he actually thought of as The Theory of Life—in capital letters. It was simple. When you didn't like something, you did it until you liked it.

Dunc thought he was crazy. "So what about getting sick," Dunc asked him, "or hitting your thumb with a hammer?"

"Same thing," Amos had told him. "If you want to learn to like it, you just put your thumb on a rock and start hitting it with a hammer. It might take a while, but you'll come to love it."

"You're nuts."

Amos didn't care. He believed in it. "You get your better brand of immunities that way. It's called the doing-it-immunities. I got it from my uncle Alfred—the one who picks his feet? He's never been sick a day in his life, and he swears by it."

"He swears about everything."

"Still . . ."

Amos had always hated spicy food, couldn't stand to sprinkle even a little pepper on it, and was applying his theory to eating the chili dog.

He turned bright red. "It's the sauce with the little seeds in it that's bad. If you swallow the seeds whole, they don't hurt, but if you bite them . . ."

He trailed off and took another gulp of Coke and a deep breath while Dunc shook his head.

"So," Amos gasped. "What have you figured out?"

Dunc neatly stuffed his napkin and paper hot-dog holder into his empty paper Coke cup and shrugged. "I said I think I'm starting to figure things out, but it's not all clear to me yet."

"Well, that's good, because nothing is clear to me—I haven't the slightest idea what you're talking about." Amos wadded his trash into a ball and threw it at the trash barrel, missed, picked it up and tried a hook shot, missed, picked it up and stood over the barrel and dropped it, and a gust of wind blew it sideways and he missed again. He finally picked it up, leaned over the barrel, and threw the cup and napkin straight down as hard as he could. It went in. "Two points."

"The problem is, we aren't covering enough ground," Dunc said, flipping his own trash cup over his shoulder to fall delicately into the exact center of the barrel.

Amos turned from the trash in disgust. "I still don't have any idea what you're talking about."

"What's going on here at the circus." He turned to face Amos. "I need more information, more data, and we aren't covering enough ground."

"Oh, man, give it a rest!"

"What do you mean?"

Amos held his hands up. "You're always seeing mysteries in everything. There's nothing strange going on in this circus unless you count some of the men working for it. It's just a tacky old circus getting tired and run down."

Dunc shook his head. "No. There's something else going on here, something I can't quite pin down. Something just . . . that . . . little . . . bit wrong."

"Right," Amos said. "Like when the parrot made me swear a lot and talked to us and told us about a buried treasure, and we wound up blowing half the town away for some moldy wheat—that little bit wrong?"

"No."

"Or when you got me snotted by a rotweiler?"

"No."

"Well, then—admit that you're wrong this time and that nothing strange is happening."

Dunc shook his head. "I can't. I just know it, Amos—there's something odd happening here, and I can't figure it out. We need more information."

"We? *I* don't have a problem. *I* don't think there's anything wrong happening. Why do *we* have a problem?"

"Because we're partners—I'm helping you on the trapeze, and you're helping me on this."

Which of course was true and Amos knew it was true—they were partners, best friends for life—and Amos knew he was going to help, knew he had to help.

"All right." He sighed. "What do you need?"

Dunc went back to the table and sat down, using his fingers to make imaginary diagrams. "The secret to everything, about everything, is knowledge. I have a feeling that something is going wrong, but we need to spread out our efforts and learn more."

"How do I spread out my effort?"

Dunc smiled. "Not like that. We've been working together, and what I mean is, we should split up. You work one side of the circus and I'll work the other, then we'll get together this evening and compare notes." He dug in the back pocket of his jeans and pulled out a small notebook and a stub of a pencil. "Just write down anything that looks a little odd to you, all right?"

Amos nodded. "Sounds good to me."

Which turned out, all in all, to be just about the biggest mistake he'd ever made.

Chapter · 7

The plan initially worked so well that Amos literally didn't see Dunc for nearly two hours.

Dunc had headed for the big top, and Amos had moved toward the sideshow tents. Both boys pointedly and carefully avoided anything to do with the animal enclosure and the wrong ends of the animals.

Amos stopped next to the banner advertising the sword swallower and the fire eater, looking up at the paintings.

They look, he thought, *as if I'd painted them myself.* The paintings on the banners showed a man about to swallow a sword longer than he was, painted as if it had been done with poster paint and a thick brush. Next to it, a man who looked very similar was about to shove a flaming torch down his throat while a girl—or it could have been a car or a lamp (Amos couldn't be sure)—looked on in horror.

He shook his head. Farther down the banner, there was a painting showing what was called the smallest horse in the world. Amos thought it could also be a duck or an alligator with its tail cut off or a really sick chicken or even a parrot. (He knew rather more than he wanted to know about parrots since his run-in with the treasure-hunting variety.) And beyond that was a painting of what could have been either a bowling ball with a neck and head or a black hole with lettering that proclaimed: UNKNOWN SPECIES! SEE IT ON THE INSIDE!

Amos shook his head and took a step to leave—he wanted little to do with the sideshow—when the whole banner system—poles, signs, and all—wavered once, twice, and fell over directly on top of him.

"Wh—"

Amos went down beneath canvas, poles,

and paintings of ruptured ducks bowling balls.

For a moment he was confused, couldn't seem to find his way out. Then he heard a voice.

"Not to worry, everything will be all right, just fine, don't worry."

A large hand came under the canvas, caught Amos by the back of his T-shirt, and plucked him out into the sun.

"See? Right as rain, right as rain."

Amos found himself looking at a man with dark hair, an almost perfectly square face and head, and a lower jaw like a bear trap.

"Clive," the man said, holding out his hand for a shake. "Clive Haskins, but they call me The Throat. I swallow things. Swallow lots of things."

He reached down, took a handful of dirt, put it in his mouth, and swallowed. "See?"

Oh, Amos thought—*oh good. Another circus person.* Of course they were all circus people, and maybe it would be nice to just meet a normal person, but no, here was Clive, another circus person.

"Just pick them up and swallow them.

That's how I got started when I was a kid. Swallowing things. Be walking along, see a bug—bam! Pick it up and swallow it. See a nickel—bam, swallow it. See a pretty marble —bam, swallow it. Here, hold this rope."

He handed a rope to Amos, who was wondering just how odd things had to be before he wrote them in the notebook for Dunc. *Note one: I met a man who swallows things. Sees a bug—bam, swallows it. Sees a quarter—bam, swallows it. Sees a parrot—bam. . . .* He shook his head.

"You a rousty?" Clive asked.

"I don't know," Amos said, shrugging. "What's a rousty?"

"Roustabout—you know, helper. You a helper?"

Amos nodded. "I was just on my way to work on the—"

"Never mind that. I need help setting up the geek show. You can do it."

"What's a geek show?" Amos looked around, half expecting to see a bunch of geeks coming at him.

"This—the sideshow. They call it a geek

show because that's what they used to show—
a geek."

"Just exactly," Amos asked slowly, "what
is a geek?"

Clive snorted. "Man, you kids don't know
nothing."

I know enough not to swallow dirt, Amos
thought, but he remained quiet.

"Geeks was wild men, kid." He rolled his
eyes and pretended to be crazy. "Wild men
from the Borneo jungles. They sat in a cage
with a chicken, and when the crowd was
pitched right, they'd grab the chicken and bite
the head off it."

So that, Amos thought, *is what my sister
means when she calls me a geek.*

" 'Course they didn't swallow it," Clive said
sarcastically. "They just bit it off and spit it
out. Your basic geek or even your top-line
geek wouldn't hold a candle to a good swallower."

"Oh." Amos was again working mentally
on the notes. *Geeks, chickens, swallowers.*

"It's the puking." Clive pulled the banner
up and tied a rope off.

"Pardon?"

"It's the puking that makes the difference. Some will get sick when a man bites the head off a chicken, but to really make them puke, you got to swallow a sword. It's a real gagger."

Maybe, Amos thought, *if I go away quietly . . .*

"Proudest I ever been was when I had a full ten banger. Ten people, and all ten blew chow. Let's see a geek top that!"

All the time he was talking, Clive kept working, and the banner was now fully back up and tied down.

"Come inside the tent." He moved back into the tent, and Amos followed. He didn't want to follow, he was sure something awful would happen if he followed, was sure he would be a gagger if he followed, but he followed just the same. He couldn't help it.

But inside Clive just helped him set up panels to make booth areas for each sideshow. There were no other acts around, and when he had finished helping, Clive waved him away. "Go help somebody else. You got to keep moving, you want to be a circus man—got to keep moving. Of course, if you want to stay and learn how to swallow, I could teach you."

Amos shook his head. "No—I'm not cut out for it."

Clive looked at him suspiciously. "You ain't a geek, are you?"

Only if you ask my sister, Amos thought, but he shook his head. "No. I'm just a rousty and maybe going to be a trapeze person."

"Fallers," Clive said. "That's what they are. Do good until they slip, then they're fallers. Splatter all over the place. Biggest mess you ever saw. No, you want job security, you got to be a swallower. . . ."

He was still mumbling as Amos moved around the corner of the tent, took two steps, and ran face-first into a man's chest.

"Watch where you're going, kid."

Amos looked up and found himself staring directly into the eyes of Blades.

Chapter · 8

Amos gulped, wondering if that made him a genetic swallower. "Nothing."

"You rousting?"

Amos nodded. "I was helping put up the geek—I mean, the sideshow."

Blades studied Amos. It was, Amos thought, about like a snake studying a frog it was about to eat. Oh great. Another swallowing joke.

"It doesn't look to me like you're doing anything. Come on."

Blades waved Amos to follow and moved off down the midway away from the big top to where some men seemed to be working. They all looked like Blades. Dirty jeans, dirty T-shirts, hair back in ducktails with lots of grease, scuffed and dirty engineer boots. All of them, every one including Blades, had a cigarette hanging from the side of his mouth.

They were putting up a canvas wall to shield the side of the circus from people who would try to get in without paying, and when Blades approached them with Amos, one of the men laughed.

"Hey, Blades—we're almost done. What do you want us to do?"

Blades looked at what they had been doing and shook his head. "Naw, it's all wrong. Tear it down and do it over."

"But—" Amos started to say. Even with no experience, he could tell the job was done right and would force people to go through the ticket booth.

"But what?" Blades turned on him, his eyes flattened into narrow slits, the smoke from his cigarette passing in front of them. "Have you got something to say?"

Amos shook his head. Quickly. "No. Not me. I'm fine. I was all wrong. I can see how it needs to be done over."

"Then you do it."

"What?"

"We're going to take a break. You take down this whole canvas wall and put it up again the right way." While he spoke, he moved from tie rope to tie rope, untying them and letting them drop until there was nothing holding the curtain up. It wobbled back and forth and fell to the ground in a crumpled heap. "There. And I expect it to be done when I get back, understand?"

He waved at the other men, and they left Amos standing there looking at the canvas and poles.

"It's impossible," he muttered. Even with three or four men it would have been hard. Alone, it simply couldn't be done.

And it didn't have to be done. It didn't make any sense. The wall had been up perfectly, and Blades had just been making more work to do.

Because he doesn't like me, Amos thought. But the truth was, Blades didn't know him, and he probably didn't like anybody very much. Probably had dreams about doing things to all the people he didn't like. Probably turned them into frogs, and . . .

He shook his head.

It wasn't just Blades. All the men must be involved in whatever it was, or they would have been mad when Blades knocked the wall down. They did all the work of putting it up and just laughed when he knocked it down.

It didn't make any sense.

He looked around, hoping to see Dunc come walking up. Dunc might know what was happening, what this all meant. That was the sort of thing Dunc did the best. Figuring things.

But he wasn't there. Amos was alone with an impossible job in an impossible situation that didn't make any logical sense. He frowned, thinking of what Dunc had said to do. What was it?

Oh yes, the notebook. He had to keep track of all these weird things.

He took the notebook out of his pocket and the stub of pencil and began to write: *Men doing work over they don't need to do.* He thought a moment, then added: *Men not doing work at all?*

So intent had he been on writing that he didn't realize he wasn't standing alone. Somebody had come up on his side and was reading over his shoulder.

"What's this—you writing a book, kid?"

Amos looked up to see Blades again.

It was impossible. He had just walked away in the opposite direction and yet here he was—he must have run around the big top to come up in back of him that way.

"Just some ideas I had." Amos flipped the notebook shut and started to put it back in his pocket. "I haven't had time to start on the curtain."

"Not so fast. Let me see that." Blades grabbed for the notebook, but Amos jerked it away and took off.

He made four steps, and Blades caught him by the back of the shirt and pulled him up, clawed the notebook out of his hand, and held Amos kicking under one arm while he read what Amos had written.

"I thought so."

"Thought so what?"

"I thought you and that other brat were spies. Are they on to us?"

"I don't know what you're talking about."

"Sure you don't. You just happen to be where I'm working, and you take a note like this, and you don't know what's happening? Let me change the question. How long have the Bobbsey Twins known what's going on?"

"Bobbsey Twins?"

"Willy and Billy—the two do-gooders who own this pile of junk they call a circus. How long?"

"I really don't know what—"

Blades shook him, once, and it felt as if his eyeballs were going to fall out.

"Talk, kid!"

"If I knew anything, I would tell you. Honest."

Blades ignored him and started walking, Amos tucked under his arm like a suitcase.

"Where are we going?"

"Where you and the other little monster won't cause any more trouble."

Which, Amos thought as Blades carried him around the end of the big top and toward the small enclosed area—which didn't sound good at all.

Chapter · 9

Blades threw Amos into the back end of a camper shell that was sitting on top of an ancient pickup parked near the back edge of the animal enclosure.

"*Oooofff!*"

Amos landed face-first in a pile of dirty T-shirts and socks mixed with empty bean cans and part of what he thought might be an antique slice of pizza.

He rolled over and sat up, then pulled himself up onto the small bench next to the table.

The inside of the camper looked about like Amos thought the inside of Blades's camper should look—a dump. There were empty beer cans and food containers everywhere, and six or seven used tubes of hair grease thrown on the floor mixed in with other dirty laundry.

He heard a key in the lock and realized that Blades had locked him in the camper. This alarmed him until he saw that the window over the table was broken out and it would be a simple matter to slip across the table and out the window.

He climbed onto the table and stuck his head out.

"Get back in, kid."

One of Blades's men—he could have doubled for Blades himself—was standing by the window.

Amos ducked back in.

There was another window over the double bunk, and he clambered up onto the bunk, but the same man could see that window as well.

Amos moved back down to the table and sat on the bench.

A cockroach that seemed the size of a small puppy crawled off a chewed piece of chicken on a paper plate on the table, and Amos slid farther off to the side.

Well, he thought, it was bad, but it

wouldn't be long. He was supposed to meet Dunc, and when he didn't show, Dunc would come looking for him and probably call the police, and before long the whole place would be upside down.

He stopped thinking as a key clicked into the lock and the door opened and Dunc came barreling in to land in the same place as Amos had landed.

"Oh, man," Dunc said, sitting up, "this is disgusting."

"You think that's bad—wait until you see the cockroach. You could ride him."

"How long have you been here?" Dunc asked.

"Just a few minutes. I was figuring you'd come to rescue me."

Dunc ignored the dig. "I've figured it out."

"Figured what out?"

"What's going on here. It threw me for a little while because what seemed to be happening wasn't really happening and only *seemed* to be happening, but once I gathered some data—"

"Dunc."

"—the data backed up my calculations

completely. It's just that I had a little initial confusion because the data indicated what it didn't really *seem* to indicate—"

"I'm going to kill you and feed you to the roaches if you don't stop and tell me what you're talking about."

Dunc stopped. "I'm telling you."

"So I can understand it."

Dunc sighed. "Well, look—what did you find out before they caught you?"

"Nothing."

"No, really. What did you see?"

"Nothing."

"What did you put in your notebook?"

"Oh. Something I didn't understand. I just said the men seemed to be working but weren't really working or doing work over they didn't need to do over."

"My point exactly!"

"It is?"

"Sure. Don't you see what it means?"

Amos looked out the window where the sun shone off the greasy head of the man guarding the camper. "No. I don't."

"Why would they do something over and over?"

"Maybe because they're stupid? I mean, some of these guys are pretty bad—right down there with bacteria and one-celled animals."

"It's to ruin the circus."

"What?"

"Sure. It's simple once you figure it out. They do work over and over, seem to work when they aren't, but in the end they get it done, or pretty much get it done. And Willy and Billy told us they were having trouble financially."

"You got all this from seeing the men work the way they work?"

Dunc smiled. "Not exactly. I overheard two of them talking about how they were pretty close to ruining the circus so some other guys could buy it out cheap. But when I heard that, it was easier to put it all together."

"So you weren't all that far ahead of me." Amos moved to the front of the camper and looked out the window. "The trick is, what are we going to do about it?"

"We have to get away and tell Willy and Billy."

Amos pointed outside. "That guy is still out there watching."

Dunc lifted an incredibly filthy curtain and nodded. "I see."

"So what do we do?" Amos looked at his watch. "They're going to start selling tickets soon. Melissa will be there, and the trapeze acts are first, right after the entrance parade. I have to get my tights from the service trailer and put them on and get into the tent before it all starts."

Dunc stared at him. "Are you still talking about doing the trapeze?"

Amos nodded. "It's bound to work. I'll be the only one up there, and she can't help but see me."

"I thought the elephant would have changed your mind a bit. He threw you close to two hundred feet."

Amos shrugged. "I don't remember much except a kind of swirling of things—like the ground above me and the sky below. But it doesn't matter anyway. I'm going to do this or die trying."

"That's what I'm worried about. That second part."

Amos ignored him. "So think up a way to get out of here. I have barely enough time to get into my tights."

"It's not possible."

"Sure it is. It's like putting on a big stocking. I watched the gymnasts in the locker room one time. You just stick a foot in and kind of peel them on."

"No. I mean getting away. That guy is watching like a hawk."

"Come on, Dunc. Quit fooling around. You *always* know what to do."

"Not this time. We're locked up, and the only way out is to risk getting caught while we do it. We wouldn't get ten feet."

"Oh man." Amos shook his head. "I don't believe you. All we need is a little razzle-dazzle and some frown-thinking by you, and we'd be right out of here. All you have to do is think of a diversion, catch the guy's attention, while one of us gets away and goes for help."

Dunc snapped his fingers. "I have an idea."

Amos smiled. "Great. What is it?"

"We just create a diversion, catch the

guard's attention, and one of us gets away to go for the authorities."

"Sounds good to me." Amos nodded. "You create the diversion, and I'll escape."

"Why you?"

"I run faster because I'm more afraid, and if I don't get away soon, I won't make the trapeze act."

"Oh. Yeah. All right."

Dunc moved to the window again and studied the guard for a moment. The man took a pack of cigarettes from the rolled-up sleeve of his T-shirt—which showed a tattoo of a snake swallowing a small town—and began to light it with a match that he flicked with his thumbnail.

This simple act provided the diversion needed—actually, more than they needed.

When the guard flicked the wooden match with his thumbnail, it flared up, and he started to light the cigarette with it. But part of the phosphorous head of the match stuck beneath his thumbnail and lit as well the main part of the match head.

Which effectively cooked the tip-end of his thumb to a well-done state and sent daggers of pain shooting up his arm to his brain. Even his not-too-bright intellect knew about pain, and he let out a bloodcurdling scream and started running in circles holding his hand.

"Now"—Dunc turned to Amos—"out the window over the sink. Hurry!"

Amos stood on the small bench and dived for the window. The glass part had been pushed open, but the screen was there.

Amos took the screen with him, landed on the ground outside in a rolling ball, and was up and running before he had time to think of getting rid of the screen, which was still around his face and kept him from seeing.

At a dead run he drove the top of his head straight into the support arm of a rearview mirror on another truck parked nearby, and his mind exploded in colors and stopped thinking of anything and everything except pumping his legs and running.

Amos was on full automatic.

Chapter · 10

It was probably just as well that Amos was running on full automatic. Things happened that he was better off not knowing.

He moved fast. Years of answering the phone through disaster after disaster, trying to make it on that all-important first ring, had given him skills far beyond those of normal people. On more than one occasion he had dreamed that he was answering the phone and awakened to find that he had run out of his room, down the stairs, through the living room, and picked up the real phone to answer the dream ring—all without awakening.

Nobody, not even Dunc, could catch him.

While the guard was still running around in little circles, Amos ricocheted off the mirror, hesitated while his thinking stopped and his instincts took over, and within two steps was again running full speed.

He cut to the right through the area where the campers were parked, catching his form and pulling it into a near classic movement—knees well up, spit flying out of the side of his mouth, eyes glazed and straight ahead (normal, although this time it was from the blow to his head)—and ran full on into Blades.

"Hey! How'd you get out?"

Amos didn't hear him, and there was no way Blades could slow him down or catch him.

He bounced off Blades, knocking him down, and was out of sight between cars in an instant.

Dunc was in back of Amos, not gaining but moving with good speed, so fast that he ran up to Blades just as the man was getting up. Dunc was moving too fast to turn, and at the last possible instant he jumped, trying to clear Blades, but he was just a bit too low, and his foot came down directly on top of Blades's head.

Dunc compensated, lunged, putting all his weight on Blades's head, and powered over, jamming Blades's head down between his shoulders so hard that Blades's eyes crossed, and he dropped on his face.

The lunge slowed Dunc. He had been almost holding his own with Amos, but now the half-beat required to push Blades's head down into his chest caused Dunc to lose two steps, and when he looked up, Amos was gone.

Still, Dunc thought it was not so bad. But he had not seen Amos hit the mirror bracket, did not know Amos was running on automatic.

Dunc remembered the plan and assumed Amos would go for the authorities, try to find the police.

The security guard.

There was a security guard by the ticket booth to keep people in line, and Dunc was sure that was where Amos would go.

He gave up following Amos and cut to the left, headed for the ticket booth to find Amos and tell the security guard what was happening.

It was too late.

When Dunc rounded the corner of the big top, he found the front area jammed with people. The crowds waiting for tickets were packed back to the parking lot, and Dunc couldn't see either the security guard or Amos anywhere.

He stood on a small stool for a few minutes, scanning the crowd, but he still didn't see anything and was about to jump down when he recognized somebody.

Melissa.

She was getting her ticket and moving to the front opening on the tent.

And he knew.

Seeing Melissa triggered his thinking and he knew.

Amos wasn't coming to look for the security guard.

Something must have happened. There hadn't been time, or he got his wires crossed, and Amos would go to the service truck and then head for the trapeze.

Dunc knew.

He wheeled around, cut in front of the crowd, and ran into the tent just as Melissa passed through the opening with the rest of the crowd.

Of all the directions where Dunc didn't want to look for Amos, most of all he didn't want to look up.

He looked up.

There, standing on the small platform near the top of the tent, holding on with one hand and waving down at the crowd, smiling widely —his eyes still vacant—glittering in spangly tights that caught light from the lights aimed at him and only looked a little bit tacky and worn; there bigger than life, there what seemed hundreds of feet above the ground . . .

There stood Amos.

"Oh," Dunc said—whispered to himself. "Oh no. Amos. Not really. Don't do this, Amos." He'd have to get Amos down, get him down without hurting him, but even as he thought it, he saw how impossible it would be.

Amos was near the top of the center pole on the small stand, his head up close to the canvas of the roof, and the only way up to him was right up the center of the pole on a small ladder.

Dunc would have to get to the center of the tent and climb the ladder and somehow drag Amos back down against his will.

Just impossible.

Still, Dunc thought, they were best friends for life. He had to try.

Dunc made his way through the crowds, which were already taking their seats while the small band—Willy and Billy with trumpets—finished the fanfare. Willy jumped from the bandstand out into the middle of the ring and took a microphone from a stand.

"Ladeeees and gentlemen! Welcome to the Classic Grand Old Circus! Before the grand entrance parade, hold on to your hats and watch the top of the tent—"

Dunc was at the pole. He grabbed the metal rungs of the ladder and started climbing.

"—for our first act. The death-defying high-bar trapeze performed by the bravest of the brave, a young man from your own home town. His name is Am—"

The microphone cut out. Willy kept talking

and hit it with his hand, but Amos's name was lost.

Dunc was at the platform. *Don't look down,* he thought—*just don't look down.* His hand was reaching up on the platform, was an inch from Amos's ankle.

"Amos!" Dunc yelled. "Amos, don't do this!"

Billy ran back to the bandstand and picked up his trumpet and joined Willy, and the music swelled higher and higher, and Amos nodded, grabbed the bar with both hands.

"No! Amos, don't! You don't know what you're doing!"

Amos stepped off into space.

Chapter · 11

Dunc scrambled up onto the platform, still not looking down, just in time to see Amos swinging, growing smaller as he swung away.

Maybe, Dunc thought, *if I don't look, maybe it won't happen.*

But he had to look, and Dunc was stunned to find Amos doing everything perfectly. He acted as if he'd been doing trapeze acts all his life.

Amos swung away with almost perfect rhythm, arching his back and kicking to make the bar go higher.

Dunc stole a quick look down at the crowd, and they had gone silent and all had their faces up, hundreds of silent faces watching Amos. Just in back of the bandstand, Dunc thought he could see Melissa.

Amos finished the swing out, kicked up at the canvas of the top of the tent, and started back. On the way back toward Dunc he curled up and stuck his legs through and hung by his knees.

The crowd oohed.

Amos's swing brought him close to Dunc, and Dunc made a grab but missed. For a moment Amos hung at the top of the swing, upside down, facing Dunc, and his eyes were still glazed.

He started the swing back, the speed picking up rapidly, and halfway through the swing he suddenly straightened his legs and dropped to hang by his ankles and feet wrapped around the ropes.

The crowd gasped.

Dunc looked down and saw that Melissa was standing, one hand to her mouth. Well, he thought, Amos had gotten her attention.

It was on the fourth swing back that things began to go wrong.

Perhaps because of the wind rushing past

his face, or just the passage of time—whatever the reason, the dazed condition wore off.

Amos swung back toward Dunc, hanging by his heels, and as he came up to Dunc, his eyes cleared and he recognized his friend.

"Dunc, what's happening?"

He looked down.

His eyes came back to Dunc, wide with fear and horror. Amos was at the top of the swing, pausing before the swing down again, hanging full down so his face was even with Dunc.

"What am I doing here?"

He started the swing back.

"Hellllllllllppp!"

Except that this time he was not in good form, not classic at all.

He was like meat on a hook.

The trapeze bar swung away, then back, then away again like a pendulum and back, and each time it went less and less until it hung straight down over the center of the ring, over the net.

With Amos hanging by his ankles below it.

"You've got to swing, Amos!" Dunc yelled.

"Swing a little and get back to where I can grab you!"

Amos hung silently.

"Just a little, Amos—just swing a little."

Amos didn't move. He hung upside down, looking over at Dunc, then at the ground, then back at Dunc.

"Come on, Amos."

Amos's ankles slipped a bit.

"Reach up and grab the bar!" Dunc yelled. "You're slip—"

Amos dropped.

Like an arrow, like a shot, like seven pounds of garbage in a three-pound bag, like a spear heading for a target Amos dropped exactly straight, head down, perfect, and hit the net at about seventy-two miles an hour, arrow-true, with his face.

For half a second it seemed that he would go through. The net plunged with him, down and down until Amos's nose was exactly two inches from the dirt of the floor of the ring.

Then the spring ties at the corners of the net took over and snapped him back up with a force very nearly equal to the speed with which he'd come down.

Except that his body had angled over, and he did not head straight back up. Instead, he went off at a forty-five-degree angle, arms and legs flailing in a great cartwheel, up over and off the net, across the side of the ring, wheeling end-over-end to land in a heap.

Directly beneath the elephant Biboe, who was waiting to do his bit with the entrance parade.

It was all too much for Biboe. First the business of Amos running beneath him earlier, and now he came flying out of nowhere and landed in a cloud of dust and animal droppings.

Biboe snaked his trunk back and down and wrapped it around Amos's middle and flicked him like a booger, back cartwheeling through the air, across the bandstand, across Willy and Billy into Melissa's lap.

The bleachers couldn't take the sudden strain, and Amos and Melissa went through, down in a pile with eight or ten people on top of them in a cloud of dirt and dust and popcorn.

All this time, Dunc had been coming down the ladder. He arrived just in time to see

Amos push his head out of the pile of splintered boards and tangled people, look up, and say:

"Was it too showy?"

Before he passed out.

Chapter · 12

Amos raised his face and aimed it at Dunc. "So what do you think—are the lines gone?"

They were at Dunc's house, in Dunc's room. Dunc was working on a model of a World War II fighter plane. He was just finishing it, and the workmanship was, as usual, perfect. No extra glue, all the joints tight and sanded smooth. Perfect. Amos was also working on a model—same war, different fighter. His model looked like a blop of glue with a piece of plastic stuck to it.

But Amos wasn't talking about the model. He was talking about his face. It had been a week since the circus disaster—as Dunc and

81

the newspapers thought of it—and Amos was worried about the grid lines in his face. When he hit the net face first, the cords had made deep impressions and left him looking like a waffle with eyes.

"The lines are almost gone." Dunc set his model on the desk.

"Good—I want the lines all gone before I call Melissa and apologize."

Dunc shook his head. "I don't think that would be a good idea."

"Why not? We saved the circus, didn't we?"

"Well . . . yes. We told Willy and Billy, and they fired the guys who were trying to ruin them. So we sort of saved the circus."

"And I did the trapeze like I said I would, didn't I?"

Dunc stared at him. "That's where the trouble starts. You didn't exactly *do* the trapeze."

"I most certainly did! Willy and Billy both said it was the greatest trapeze act they'd ever seen."

"No." Dunc shook his head. "What they said was it was the most incredible trapeze act they'd ever seen."

"It means the same thing."

"Not exactly."

"Close enough for me to call Melissa."

"Amos, you broke her ankle when you fell on her."

"I didn't fall—Biboe threw me."

"Still—"

"And I didn't mean to break her ankle. It was an accident. And that's what I want to apologize for—she's just waiting for me to call. I can feel it."

Dunc leaned across the desk. "Look, Amos. She didn't catch your name. She said if she ever found out who broke her ankle, she was going to break *his* ankle, and then his neck. The way it is now, she doesn't know you—in other words, it's normal. If you tell her your name, it's all over."

He was going to say more, was going to tell Amos that it was better to be wise and wait— maybe until he was sixty or so. He was going to try and help Amos through this difficult time, was going to do all that he could—except that the phone rang.

Amos's nostrils flared, his head swiveled, his teeth bared.

"No, Amos. It's not your house. She couldn't know you were here."

It didn't help. Well before the second ring, showing excellent form even if there was a slight waffle look still on his face, knees pumping, spit flying out the side of his mouth—

Amos was off.

Be sure to join Dunc and Amos in these other Culpepper Adventures:

The Case of the Dirty Bird

When Dunc Culpepper and his best friend, Amos, first see the parrot in a pet store, they're not impressed—it's smelly, scruffy, and missing half its feathers. They're only slightly impressed when they learn that the parrot speaks four languages, has outlived ten of its owners, and is probably 150 years old. But when the bird starts mouthing off about buried treasure, Dunc and Amos get pretty excited—let the amateur sleuthing begin!

Dunc's Doll

Dunc and his accident-prone friend, Amos, are up to their old sleuthing habits once again. This time they're after a band of doll thieves! When a doll that once belonged to Charles Dickens's daughter is stolen from an exhibition at the local mall, the two boys put on their detective gear and do some serious snooping. Will a vicious watchdog keep them from retrieving the valuable missing doll?

Culpepper's Cannon

Dunc and Amos are researching the Civil War cannon that stands in the town square when they find a note inside telling them about a time portal. Entering it through the dressing room of La Petite, a women's clothing store, the boys find themselves in downtown Chatham on March 8, 1862—the day before the historic clash between the *Monitor* and the *Merrimac*. But the Confederate soldiers they meet mistake them for Yankee spies. Will they make it back to the future in one piece?

Dunc Gets Tweaked

Dunc and Amos meet up with a new buddy named Lash when they enter the radical world of skateboard competition. When somebody "cops"—steals—Lash's prototype skateboard, the boys are determined to get it back. After all, Lash is about to shoot for a totally rad world's record! Along the way they learn a major lesson: *Never* kiss a monkey!

Dunc's Halloween

Dunc and Amos are planning the best route to get the most candy on Halloween. But their plans change when Amos is slightly bitten by a werewolf. He begins scratching himself and chasing UPS trucks—he's become a were-puppy!

Dunc Breaks the Record

Dunc and Amos have a small problem when they try hang-gliding—they crash in the wilderness. Luckily Amos has read a book about a boy who survived in the wilderness for fifty-four days. Too bad Amos doesn't have a hatchet. Things go from bad to worse when a wild man holds the boys captive. Can anything save them now?

Dunc and the Flaming Ghost

Dunc's not afraid of ghosts, although Amos is sure that the old Rambridge house is haunted by the ghost of Blackbeard the Pirate. Then the best friends meet Eddie, a meek man who claims to be impersonating Blackbeard's ghost in order to live in the house in peace. But if that's true, why are flames shooting from his mouth?

Amos Gets Famous

Deciphering a code they find in a library book, Amos and Dunc stumble onto a burglary ring. The burglars' next target is the home of Melissa, the girl of Amos's dreams (who doesn't even know that he's alive). Amos longs to be a hero to Melissa, so nothing will stop him from solving this case—not even a mind-boggling collision with a jock, a chimpanzee, and a toilet.